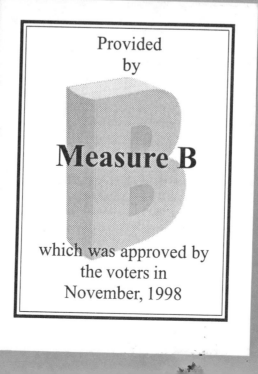

Provided
by

Measure B

which was approved by
the voters in
November, 1998

The Village of Basketeers

HOUGHTON MIFFLIN COMPANY · BOSTON 2005

Lynda Gene Rymond

The Village of Basketeers

illustrated by Nicoletta Ceccoli

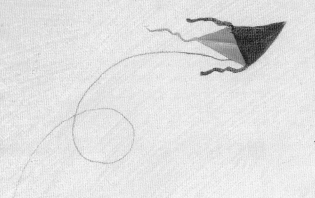

www.houghtonmifflinbooks.com

The text of this book is set in 17-point ITC Golden Cockerel
The illustrations are done using acrylics and pastels
Book design by Carol Goldenberg

Library of Congress Cataloging-in-Publication Data

Rymond, Lynda Gene.
The village of basketeers / by Lynda Gene Rymond; illustrated by Nicoletta Ceccoli.
p. cm.
Summary: As a fierce wind blows stronger and stronger through their village,
two excellent basket makers try and fail to capture it, but give two young friends,
Kip and Elsa, an idea that just might work.
ISBN 0-618-39671-3
[1. Basket making—Fiction. 2. Winds—Fiction. 3. Villages—Fiction.]
I. Ceccoli, Nicoletta, ill. II. Title.
PZ7.R984Vi 2005
[Fic]—dc22
2004009219
ISBN-13: 978-0-618-39671-9

Manufactured in China
SCP 10 9 8 7 6 5 4 3 2 1

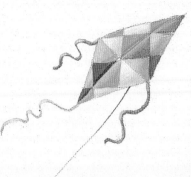

For Charles, for believing in fairytales and me
—L.G.R.

To Stefano, who makes me fly
—N.C.

Kip and Elsa lived in a small village high up on the cliffs by the sea. The sea was too rough for fishing and the soil too rocky for farming, but the tough grasses and reeds that grew by the water were perfect for making baskets. The villagers made baskets for the farming folk and fishing folk, country people and city people, and traded baskets for everything they needed. You could look at just about any basket and say, "This came from the Village of Basketeers!"

Elsa and Kip and the other children in the village first learned to make simple baskets for carrying eggs or kittens. By the time they were grownups, they would be able to weave anything — a house for a duck, a barn for a horse, or a carriage fit for a queen.

As long as the oldest person could remember, life had been good in the Village of Basketeers. Then, one day, the wind blew a little harder than it usually did. Some people didn't mind, and some people stayed inside. As Kip walked to school, his basket hat blew off and disappeared into the clouds as if it had wings. "Tomorrow this wind has got to stop," said Kip.

"I hope so," said Elsa. "Then we can look for your hat."

But by the next day, the wind blew with a roar. Mamas and papas tied their children to each other before walking them to school, and little Elsa sailed up like a kite on a string. Grownups had to fill their pockets with rocks and hold hands, and, just for safekeeping, they tied the cats to the dogs. "The weather will clear up tomorrow," the people told each other. "This wind can't last forever."

But on the third day, the wind blew harder still. It blew fish out of the sea. It blew the moon out of the clouds. School was closed and everybody stayed home. "At least we've got fish," said Kip's grandma, as she opened her door and let three shining sardines blow into her frying pan. "The weather's bound to change. Weather always does."

But on the fourth day, the wind blew stronger than ever. It was almost impossible to hear over the roar. The mayor of the village called a meeting. To get there, people held on to trees and fences and each other. And on the way, they stopped to tie the cats and dogs to the horses — the wind was that strong!

Inside the meeting hall, the mayor stood up and shouted as loud as she could. "Does anyone have a good idea how to stop this wind?" The villagers shrugged. How do you stop the wind?

An old man stood up. "I've been building fish-trap baskets for years," he bellowed. "I'll weave a trap to catch the wind. I'll make it as strong as iron."

"Sounds like a good idea!" shouted the mayor.

For a day and a night the old man worked. The villagers cut bundles of reeds and passed them, from person to person, to where the man sat weaving the wind trap. Though it was hard to stay awake, Kip and Elsa and the other children helped. They all worked by sunlight and starlight, for it was no use trying to light a torch, and the moon had been blown out of the clouds days ago.

In the morning, the wind trap was finished. The marvelous basket was strong enough to catch a whale. The villagers cheered, then ran to tie the horses to the cows, for the wind was blowing stronger by the moment. "One, two, three!" the old man cried, throwing the trap open.

The wind sailed into the basket with a howl. It picked up the trap and the basketeer who'd made it and sent them flying up into the clouds where the moon used to be. The villagers moaned.

"Time for another meeting!" called the mayor.

Everyone gathered in the meeting hall, and the mayor shouted above the roaring wind, "Does anyone else have a good idea?" The people shrugged. Who can change the weather?

A tall woman stood up and stretched her arms wide, as if she were measuring an elephant. "I have woven basket barns all my life," she hollered. "Maybe I could weave a barn as big as a mountain, big enough to hold the wind."

"Sounds like a good idea!" shouted the mayor.

The whole village worked for a day and a night and most of another day. Elsa, Kip, and the other children brought food and drink to the grownups in line, so everyone could work without rest. The barn maker's fingers darted like lightning, sweat ran down her face, and in the long night her eyes grew heavy for sleep. But all the while her fingers flew, making the biggest basket of her life.

Finally, the gigantic barn was finished. It was nearly as big as a mountain and everyone watched as the woman threw open the door. The wind sailed into the basket and with a tremendous roar blew both the barn and its maker into the clouds where the moon used to be. The people groaned and hurried to tie the cats, dogs, horses, and cows to the mightiest oak tree in the village square. Nobody said that the wind might go away tomorrow. Nobody believed it.

Elsa and Kip met in their special meeting place. Both had carried a bucket full of water to keep from blowing away.

"I miss the moon," said Elsa sadly. "She used to shine in my window so brightly that I was never afraid of the dark. There *has* to be a way to stop the wind."

"Well, big baskets don't work and strong baskets don't work, either. What else could we try?" asked Kip.

"We could try the opposite!" Elsa said. "What's the opposite of big and strong?"

"Tiny! Tiny and soft!" answered Kip.

"Yes!" said Elsa. "A tiny basket just like the ones we made when we were learning how to weave."

"And we can make it soft inside," Kip said. "With down feathers and — "

"Lamb's wool," added Elsa.

"And thistledown. Nothing is softer than thistledown," Kip said.

The two friends gathered slender grasses, young reeds, and the softest things they could find, and brought them back to the safety of the cave.

They wove a basket so small that an egg might have been bigger, and tucked in the tiniest feathers from hummingbirds and goldfinches. When it was finished, they turned it carefully in their hands. The little basket looked and felt as soft as a kitten's tummy.

"Couldn't be softer," said Kip.

"Couldn't be smaller," said Elsa.

Just then, they saw a cat and a spotted dog sail over the village into the clouds where the moon used to be. The wind was blowing harder than ever!

Kip quickly tucked the tiny basket into
his shirt, and they carried their heavy
buckets of water to the mayor's house.
The mayor rang the loudest bell in
the tower, and the entire village met
on the mountain. Everyone held on
to Kip and Elsa as, together, they
held the basket above their heads.

The wind laughed to see such a little
thing held out to catch its magnificent
power. In fact, the basket was so small
that the wind had to come up *very*
close to see it clearly.

And when the wind came close, it saw that the basket was perfectly made by tiny fingers, and it saw the down feathers and cattail fluff and thistledown. The basket looked so . . . soft. Soft and cozy. It was a cuddly place, perfect for napping, especially for something that had been blowing hard for days and days. *Soft*, the wind seemed to sigh. *Co-zzzy . . . zzzz*, it seemed to whisper. The air grew still and quiet.

The wind had stopped! The villagers wanted to shout for joy, but no one wanted to wake the sleeping wind. Kip and Elsa carried the tiny basket back to the safety of their special meeting place. Then they ran to their mamas and papas, who tossed them up in the air with a quiet "Hurray!"

The villagers untied the cats, dogs, horses, and cows from the giant oak tree, and the animals danced with happiness to be free.

Everybody celebrated, quietly playing basket drums and basket fiddles, and as the sun was setting, who should the villagers see but the two basket weavers who had been blown to the clouds where the moon used to be — walking home with the cat and spotted dog they had found along the way.

As the stars came out, the parents gathered up their children, for it was bedtime. "Good night, Elsa, good night, Kip. Thank you for stopping the wind!" the villagers called out softly.

"I miss the moon," said Elsa sleepily as her papa carried her home.

"Don't worry," he said. "She has a long way to travel."

"I miss the moon," said Elsa sadly to her mama as she got ready for bed.

"She's on her way, you'll see her soon," said Mama.

Elsa climbed into bed and looked out the window and there, coming over the hill to join the stars, was the lovely, silver-bright moon.

The End

❦